WHAT LITTLE BOYS ARE MADE OF

by Robert Neubecker

Balzer + Bray
An Imprint of HarperCollinsPublishers

What Little Boys Are Made Of
Copyright © 2012 by Robert Neubecker
All rights reserved.
Manufactured in China.
No part of this book may be used or reproduced in any manner
whatsoever without written permission except in the case of brief quotations embodied in
critical articles and reviews. For information address HarperCollins Children's Books, a
division of HarperCollins Publishers,
10 East 53rd Street, New York, NY 10022.
www.harpercollinschildrens.com

Library of Congress Cataloging-in-Publication Data is available.
ISBN 978-0-06-202355-1 (trade bdg.)

Typography by Carla Weise
12 13 14 15 16   SCP   10 9 8 7 6 5 4 3 2 1
❖
First Edition

For my mom, who fearlessly
piloted her Buick on hundreds
of missions over hostile territory,
through blazing deserts, across
polar ice, and into outer space.
She never lost a man.
—R.N.

What are little boys made of,
   made of?

What are little boys made of?

Moons and stars and rockets to Mars,

Blast and boom
    and uppity zoom!

That's what little boys are made of.

What are little boys made of?

Snakes and rats and big jungle cats,
Vines and rocks and razor-tooth crocs!

That's what little boys are made of.

What are little boys made of?

Sticks and stones
   and skulls and bones,

Ships and sails and oceans and whales!

That's what little boys are made of.

What are little boys made of?

Leap and soar
    and kick and score,
        run and jump

and bumpity-thump!

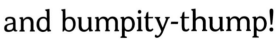

That's what little boys are made of.

What are little boys made of?

Horses and lords and knights with swords,
Wings and tails and dragons with scales!

That's what little boys are made of.

What are little boys made of, made of?

What are little boys made of?

Sugar and spice and everything nice?

Frogs and snails and puppy-dogs' tails?

A kiss and a hug,
a snuggle and
LOVE.

That's what little boys are made of!